THE
SEVEN SPECIES

Stories and Recipes
Inspired by the Foods of the Bible

MATT BIERS-ARIEL

Illustrated by
TAMA GOODMAN

UAHC Press ✦ New York, New York

For Djina, my favorite gardener.
M. B. A.

For Zelig, that your love of books, nature, and
our tradition blossom as you grow.
T. G.

Text copyright © 2003 by Matt Biers-Ariel
Illustrations copyright © 2003 by Tama Goodman

Library of Congress Cataloging-in-Publication Data

Biers-Ariel, Matt.
The seven species / Matt Biers-Ariel ; illustrated by Tama Goodman.
p. cm.
Summary: A collection of short stories celebrating the seven species of
fruits and grains grown in Israel that are held sacred by the Jewish people,
with descriptions of and recipes using each.
Contents: The teaching date—The date—Sephardic Charoset—Not
Yet—The fig—A slice of heaven—God is hungry—The Taste of
Freedom—Wheat—World's best challah—The crying tree—The
olive—Curing olives—The ivory pomegranate—The pomegranate—Festive
fall salad with pomegranate seeds—Barley brothers—Barley—Mushroom
barley soup—Kiddush—The grape—dolmas.
ISBN 0-8074-0852-2 (alk. paper)
[1. Seven species (Jewish law)—Fiction. 2. Judaism—Customs and
practices—Fiction. 3. Jews—Fiction. 4. Food—Religious aspects.]
I. Goodman, Tama, ill.   II. Title.

PZ7.B4775 Se 2002
[Fic]—dc21   2002029119

This book is printed on acid-free paper.
Manufactured in the United States of America
10 9 8 7 6 5 4 3 2 1

THE SEVEN SPECIES
Stories and Recipes
Inspired by the Foods of the Bible

CONTENTS

INTRODUCTION

For Adonai your God is bringing you into a good land, a land with streams and springs and fountains issuing from plain and hill; a land of wheat and barley, of vines, figs, and pomegranates, a land of olive trees and honey.

—Deuteronomy 8:7–8

Wheat, barley, grape, fig, pomegranate, olive, and date. Collectively they are known as the *sheva minim*, the seven species of sacred fruits and grains grown in the Land of Israel.

While Jews are widely known as the People of the Book, the ancient Israelites were a people of the land, mostly farmers and shepherds. Rather than contemplate God's sacred Torah, they contemplated God's sacred Creation. Instead of chanting from a prayer book as a means of spiritual uplift, they sacrificed offerings from their flocks and harvests. Indeed, to the ancient Israelites, the seven species were not only evidence of the land's great bounty, but evidence of God's love toward them.

After Israel's monarchies fell, the majority of Jews settled outside of Israel and became an increasingly urban people. Though many rural ways of life were forgotten, the memory of the seven sacred species stayed alive throughout the generations. Now in the modern State of Israel, Jewish farmers are once again cultivating these seven species.

Today there are Jews disconnected with Judaism who find their spiritual path in nature. Conversely, there are religious Jews who fail to notice God's handiwork in the first blossoms of spring. This book was written in the hope of uniting the People of the Book with the People of the Land through stories and natural histories about the seven species. In addition, the book contains recipes using the species, because as every Jew knows, eating is sometimes the most spiritual of endeavors.

B'tayavon!

Date

THE TEACHING DATE

In the days of old there were no schools, and it was therefore the responsibility of fathers and mothers to teach their children Torah. Some five-year-old children were able to sit and study with no problem. But others—well—this story is about one of those children.

It was time for Yishai to teach his youngest son, Baruch, the Torah of Moses. However, Baruch did not have time to sit and study with his father. He was busy playing carpenter, building pretend chairs, tables, camel saddles, and other important items.

One day Yishai managed to sit his son under a date tree with a Torah opened to Vayikra, the third book of the Torah. Why the third book first? Because children come into this world as pure souls, and the focus of Vayikra is on purity. Therefore, it is the logical place to start one's Torah study.

Yishai began by having Baruch repeat words after him.

"Vayikra," Yishai said, pointing to the first word of the book.

"Bayizra," said Baruch, looking off in the distance.

"Vayikra!" Yishai said louder, tapping his finger on the word.

"Bayizra," said Baruch, twirling a stick in the sand. Baruch was going to be a great builder. He had no need to learn Torah. Instead of concentrating on Vayikra, he was thinking about the first real project he wanted to make, a tent. Unfortunately, Baruch only knew how to build pretend items, not anything real.

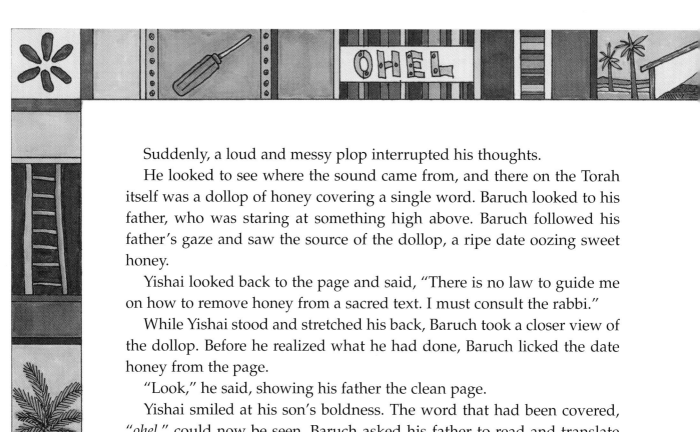

Suddenly, a loud and messy plop interrupted his thoughts.

He looked to see where the sound came from, and there on the Torah itself was a dollop of honey covering a single word. Baruch looked to his father, who was staring at something high above. Baruch followed his father's gaze and saw the source of the dollop, a ripe date oozing sweet honey.

Yishai looked back to the page and said, "There is no law to guide me on how to remove honey from a sacred text. I must consult the rabbi."

While Yishai stood and stretched his back, Baruch took a closer view of the dollop. Before he realized what he had done, Baruch licked the date honey from the page.

"Look," he said, showing his father the clean page.

Yishai smiled at his son's boldness. The word that had been covered, "*ohel*," could now be seen. Baruch asked his father to read and translate the word for him.

"*Ohel*," said Yishai. "It means tent."

"Tent?" repeated Baruch. "The Torah talks about tents?"

"The Torah teaches us about everything," Yishai replied. "Not only does it mention tents, but it contains instructions on how to build the most magnificent tent in the world, God's tent, the *mishkan*."

Baruch realized it was no accident that the honey had dripped on his special word; he knew that everything has its reason.

From that point on, Baruch became interested in words of Torah. He learned all that his father taught him. The elders of the town praised both Yishai for his teaching and Baruch for his learning. But father and son knew better. It was the honey.

When Baruch grew up, he became a great builder. When he had children of his own, he brought a jar of date honey to their first Torah lesson. Placing a dollop of honey on the page, he would instruct the child to lick it off, saying, "May your study of Torah be as sweet as this honey."

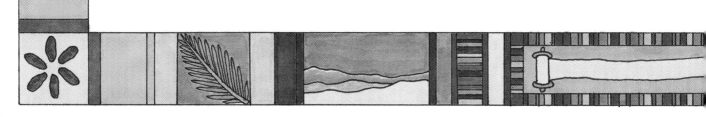

✦　✦　✦

Even today many Jewish children lick a dollop of honey off their first Jewish book, or are given chocolate at their first Jewish studies lesson, so they may associate learning Torah with sweetness.

אבגדה
וזחטי
כלמנס
עפצקר
שת

THE DATE

The date has been cultivated in Arabia and other parts of the Middle East for more than six thousand years. For people living in the desert, the sweet date is a staple food because it is plentiful and does not spoil. Besides the fruit, the date tree has many other uses. Its fiber is made into rope, its sap is distilled to make palm wine, and its leaves are used as roofing material both for houses in the desert and for sukkahs built during the holiday of Sukkot. The leaves can also be woven into mats and baskets, or used as brooms. Even the hard pits are used as animal feed.

The date palm needs a hot, sunny climate to thrive. The temperature in the growing season must be at least ninety degrees. The date palm needs little rain, but must have a constant water supply at its roots. This explains why date palms are found at many oases.

The date palm can live for one hundred years and can produce up to two hundred pounds of fruit in a season. Dates, however, are a challenging crop to farm because there are separate male and female date trees. Pollen from the male tree must be applied by hand to the flowers on the female tree. This is not a difficult task when the tree is young and small. Yet, date palms grow taller each year of their life. A typical tree can reach a height between one and two hundred feet. Pollinating a one-hundred-foot tree by hand is both time consuming and arduous.

The date (*tamar* in Hebrew) is not mentioned by name in Deuteronomy 8:8, the verse that details the seven species. Rather, the word "honey" (*d'vash* in Hebrew) is listed as one of the species. The rabbinic interpreter Rashi, basing his comments on *Targum Yonatan*, determined that the honey mentioned in this verse was not bee honey, but date honey—the syrup squeezed from ripe dates (Rashi on Exodus 34:26). Rashi and other rabbinic interpreters believed it strange to include bee honey, a product of animal manufacture, within a list of plants. Therefore, the honey must also be of plant origin.

Historically, palm fronds were carried before kings as a symbol of victory because fronds neither fall off the tree nor wither in the winter (I Maccabee 13:37, 14:4). The Christian holiday of Palm Sunday reenacts the triumphant arrival of Jesus in Jerusalem with the waving of date palm fronds (Matthew 21:8, Mark 11:8). In Solomon's Temple, the date palm was used as one of the central design motifs (I Kings 6:29). In addition to providing sukkah roofing material during the holiday of Sukkot, a single young date palm frond is used to make the *lulav* (Leviticus 23:40). In Arabic culture, the date palm is believed to be the Tree of Life. To a people living in the harsh desert climate of the Middle East, the date palm may indeed be the tree that makes life possible.

Sephardic Charoset

1 lb. pitted dates	½ tsp. ground cinnamon (optional)
1 c. water	½ tsp. ground cardamom (optional)
1 c. chopped walnuts	2 Tbsp. sweet wine (optional)

Simple, yet delicious. You may want to make a double batch in case the first batch disappears before the seder!

Put dates in water. Bring to a boil, lower heat, and simmer. Stir and mash dates while simmering. Add water if necessary. Simmer 45–60 minutes until dates turn into a paste. When the paste is cool, add walnuts and mix well. Taste. If you desire, add the spices and/or wine.

Fig

NOT YET

Joshua had fought in many wars and was sick of fighting. David, too, was often called upon to bear arms and prayed for the day when the Messiah would arrive and "beat their swords into plowshares" as the prophet Micah had written. He longed for the time when "every man would sit under his grapevine or fig tree with no one to disturb him" (Micah 4:4).

It was market day and Joshua was buying a sack of grain when he spotted the prophet Elijah. Joshua dropped the sack and ran to greet the prophet.

"Oh, Elijah," Joshua began. "I am sick and tired of war. When will the time arrive when I can sit under a fig tree in peace?"

Elijah said, "The time is now. The tree you speak of is here."

"The tree is here now?" Joshua asked, his eyes wide.

"Yes, it is here now."

"Where?"

Elijah pointed his finger. "The tree you seek can be found along the bank of the river to the west of town. Cross the bridge and walk 613 steps *upstream*. There you will find the tree you seek."

Joshua thanked Elijah and left to search for the tree.

As soon as Joshua left, David entered the market and saw Elijah. He, too, ran to greet the prophet. David asked the same question as Joshua, and Elijah gave him the same answer.

Well, almost.

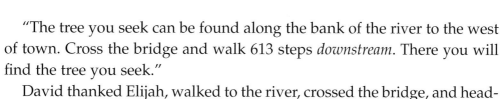

"The tree you seek can be found along the bank of the river to the west of town. Cross the bridge and walk 613 steps *downstream*. There you will find the tree you seek."

David thanked Elijah, walked to the river, crossed the bridge, and headed downstream. Sure enough, 613 steps later, David came upon a magnificent fig tree. Her strong trunk supported a large canopy of branches, leaves, and fruit. David sat down and leaned against the smooth trunk. The tree's shade cooled him from the hot sun, and a feeling of calm, a feeling of peace came over him.

"Ah," he said to himself, "so this is what the messianic age feels like."

A ripe fig fell into David's lap, and he recalled his rabbi's teaching: Why is a fig like the Torah? Because like the Torah, every part of the fig is good. The fig has no shell to peel or seed to spit out. It is all good to eat. In the Torah, there are only words of Truth; there is not a wasted word to discard.

David ate the fig, closed his eyes, and dreamed. Secrets of Torah poured into David like a pitcher of pure mountain water into a crystal glass.

Awhile later, David awoke and knew he had to share his discovery with the rest of the world. The age of the Messiah was here.

Meanwhile, Joshua had walked to the river, crossed the bridge, and headed upstream. Sure enough, 613 steps later Joshua found a beautiful fig tree. Her strong trunk supported a large canopy of branches, leaves, and fruit. Joshua sat down and leaned against the smooth trunk. The tree's shade cooled him from the hot sun, and a feeling of calm, a feeling of peace came over him.

"Ah," he said to himself, "so this is what the messianic age feels like."

A ripe fig fell into Joshua's lap, and he recalled his rabbi's teaching: Why is a fig like the Torah? Because like the Torah, every part of the fig is good. The fig has no shell to peel or seed to spit out. It is all good to eat. In the Torah, there are only words of Truth; there is not a wasted word to discard.

Joshua ate the fig, closed his eyes, and dreamed. Secrets of Torah

poured into Joshua like a pitcher of fresh spring water into a golden goblet.

After awhile, Joshua awoke and knew he had to share his discovery with the rest of the world. The age of the Messiah was here.

Joshua and David met each other on the bridge as they were running back to town.

"David, my friend," said Joshua, "I have wonderful news. War is over, the age of the Messiah is here."

"I know," said David, "I have the same news. I was just now sitting under the fig tree prophesied in the holy Bible."

"Me, too!" shouted Joshua. "I found the same tree. It's just a little upstream from here."

"Oh, my friend," said David. "The discovery has slightly confused you. The tree we speak of is downstream." David pointed in that direction.

"No, my friend. It is you who are confused. I was just there. It is that way," said Joshua pointing upstream.

"You lie," said David.

"No," said Joshua. "You lie."

"No!" yelled David, and he shoved Joshua.

Joshua shoved back and fists were flying.

On a hill above the river, Elijah watched and sighed.

"Not yet. The age of the Messiah has not yet arrived."

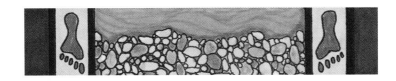

THE FIG

Fig trees are often found growing near rivers or streams. A beautiful tree possessing a strong trunk, the fig grows between fifteen and thirty feet high, creating a large shade canopy. A fresh fig is considered by many to be the most delicious of all fruits. Unfortunately, ripe figs spoil easily, so the majority of figs are dried before being shipped to market. Fig trees produce two crops each season. The first ripening usually occurs in June and July, the second in August and September.

There is historical evidence of fig cultivation from 5000 B.C.E. A text from 2900 B.C.E. speaks of the medicinal value of figs. Both the Greeks and the Romans considered the fig tree sacred. The Muslim prophet, Muhammed, said, "If I could bring one fruit to Paradise, it would be the fig."

The fig plays a major role in the story of Adam and Eve. Some biblical scholars claim that the fig tree was the Tree of Knowledge of Good and Evil. Though the forbidden fruit is commonly thought to be an apple, that is an unlikely possibility, as apples did not grow in the Middle East in biblical times. Regardless of whether or not the fig was in fact the forbidden fruit, Adam and Eve did use fig leaves to make their first clothes. Since the diameter of a fig leaf can reach ten inches, the first couple made a good choice.

A humorous story about the fig from Ecclesiastes Rabbah 2:25 concerns an old Jew who was planting a fig tree when Hadrian, the Roman emperor, walked by. Hadrian laughed at the old man. "You are one hundred years old and you plant fig trees? Do you expect to eat fruit from your tree?" "If I merit it, I shall eat. If not, I plant for my children, just as my ancestors planted for me." Hadrian told the old man that if he lived to see the trees bear figs, he should let Hadrian know. Sure enough the old man lived long enough to see his trees bear fruit, and he gathered a basket of figs to take to Hadrian. Hadrian took the figs from the basket and filled the basket with gold. When asked why he was giving such honor to an old Jew, Hadrian replied, "His Creator honors him; should I not, too?" Now the wife of the old man's neighbor told her husband that the emperor was trading baskets of figs for gold. He went to the palace with his basket of figs. The guards asked him what he was doing. The man said, "I have heard that the king loves figs and exchanges them for gold." The guards laughed and placed the man by the city gate. Everyone coming or going from the city was commanded to take a fig and throw it at the man. When the man came home and complained to his wife, she told him, "Be glad they were ripe figs and not hard."

A Slice of Heaven

Compliments of Sharon Strauss

This appetizer, which takes five minutes to prepare, is true to its name.

1 baguette
1 package goat cheese (approximately 4 oz.)
5–7 fresh figs

Slice the baguette into 1-inch rounds.
Spread cheese on rounds.
Slice figs lengthwise into thirds.
Place fig slice on top of cheese.
Pop baguette into mouth.

Wheat

GOD IS HUNGRY

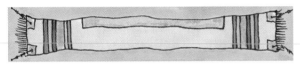 Like most Jews in the synagogue, Benjamin hung on every word of the rabbi's sermon. Yet, unlike most Jews in the synagogue, Benjamin had to strain to hear the rabbi. He was slightly deaf.

One day the rabbi pounded the lectern and shouted, "God is hungry for your prayers!"

Unfortunately, Benjamin sneezed just as the rabbi spoke. Instead of hearing, "God is hungry for your prayers," Benjamin only heard, "God is hungry."

Can it be, Benjamin thought, that God needs to eat? It sounds crazy, but didn't the ancient Israelites sacrifice goats and grain at the Temple?

Benjamin kneaded his *tzitzit*, lost in thought. Well, the rabbi knows more about God than I do, so it must be that God is hungry. And if God is hungry, I should feed God.

Benjamin went home and asked his wife, Ruth, to make an extra challah on Friday.

"It's not enough that I feed every urchin you bring home on Shabbat," Ruth said. "Now I'm feeding God." She sighed. "Plain or sesame?"

The next Friday Benjamin entered the synagogue early in the morning with a sesame challah in his hand. He wondered where to put the challah so that God would find it. He scanned the sanctuary until his eyes lit upon the ark that held the holy Torah scrolls.

Benjamin snapped his fingers. "Of course!" he exclaimed softly.

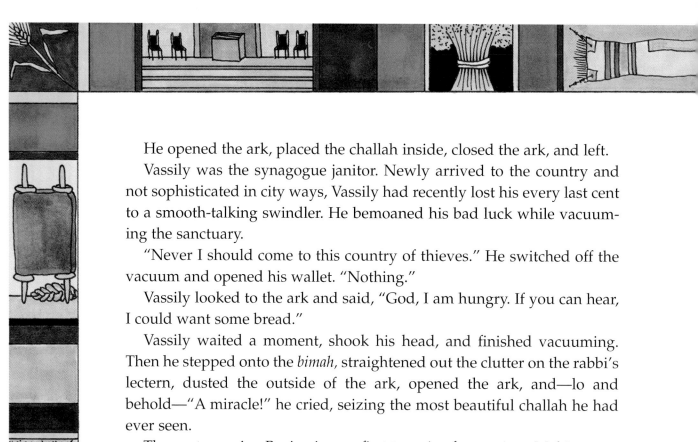

He opened the ark, placed the challah inside, closed the ark, and left.

Vassily was the synagogue janitor. Newly arrived to the country and not sophisticated in city ways, Vassily had recently lost his every last cent to a smooth-talking swindler. He bemoaned his bad luck while vacuuming the sanctuary.

"Never I should come to this country of thieves." He switched off the vacuum and opened his wallet. "Nothing."

Vassily looked to the ark and said, "God, I am hungry. If you can hear, I could want some bread."

Vassily waited a moment, shook his head, and finished vacuuming. Then he stepped onto the *bimah,* straightened out the clutter on the rabbi's lectern, dusted the outside of the ark, opened the ark, and—lo and behold—"A miracle!" he cried, seizing the most beautiful challah he had ever seen.

The next morning Benjamin was first to arrive for services. Making sure no one was watching, he stepped onto the *bimah,* gently opened the ark, and—lo and behold—"A miracle!" he cried, brushing out the crumbs that God had left.

The next four weeks followed a similar pattern. Benjamin would place a fresh challah (sometimes sesame, sometimes plain) into the ark early Friday morning. Late Friday morning Vassily would take it out.

On the sixth Friday, Benjamin put the challah in the ark. He left through the back door, and immediately Vassily came in through the side door. Vassily had business to attend to, so he needed to finish his synagogue work early. He vacuumed quickly and went to the ark. As he removed the challah, he heard a yell.

"Thief! Goniff!" cried Benjamin as he ran up the aisle. He had forgotten his hat in the synagogue. When he returned to fetch it, he caught the new janitor stealing God's challah.

Benjamin leapt onto the *bimah* and yelled, "That challah is God's!"

Vassily looked at the man and said, "This is mine."

Vassily turned to leave, but Benjamin pushed him.

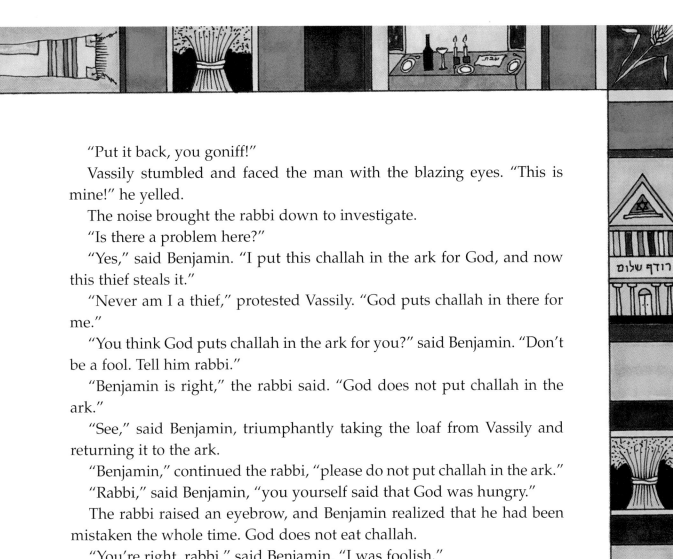

"Put it back, you goniff!"

Vassily stumbled and faced the man with the blazing eyes. "This is mine!" he yelled.

The noise brought the rabbi down to investigate.

"Is there a problem here?"

"Yes," said Benjamin. "I put this challah in the ark for God, and now this thief steals it."

"Never am I a thief," protested Vassily. "God puts challah in there for me."

"You think God puts challah in the ark for you?" said Benjamin. "Don't be a fool. Tell him rabbi."

"Benjamin is right," the rabbi said. "God does not put challah in the ark."

"See," said Benjamin, triumphantly taking the loaf from Vassily and returning it to the ark.

"Benjamin," continued the rabbi, "please do not put challah in the ark."

"Rabbi," said Benjamin, "you yourself said that God was hungry."

The rabbi raised an eyebrow, and Benjamin realized that he had been mistaken the whole time. God does not eat challah.

"You're right, rabbi," said Benjamin. "I was foolish."

"I am foolish, too," said Vassily.

The mystery was solved but everyone was sad.

Suddenly the rabbi grabbed the challah and said, "Benjamin gave the challah to God. God gave the challah to Vassily. Bypass God, and Benjamin gives the challah directly to Vassily. Benjamin, it's not God you are feeding. But by feeding Vassily, it's God's work you are doing."

Understanding slowly spread across the men's faces. Benjamin handed the challah to Vassily. Vassily took the challah.

"I thank you," said Vassily.

"You're welcome," said Benjamin. "Tonight will you join Ruth and me for Shabbat dinner? She—uh—enjoys visitors."

The two men hugged. The rabbi returned to her office.

THE TASTE OF FREEDOM

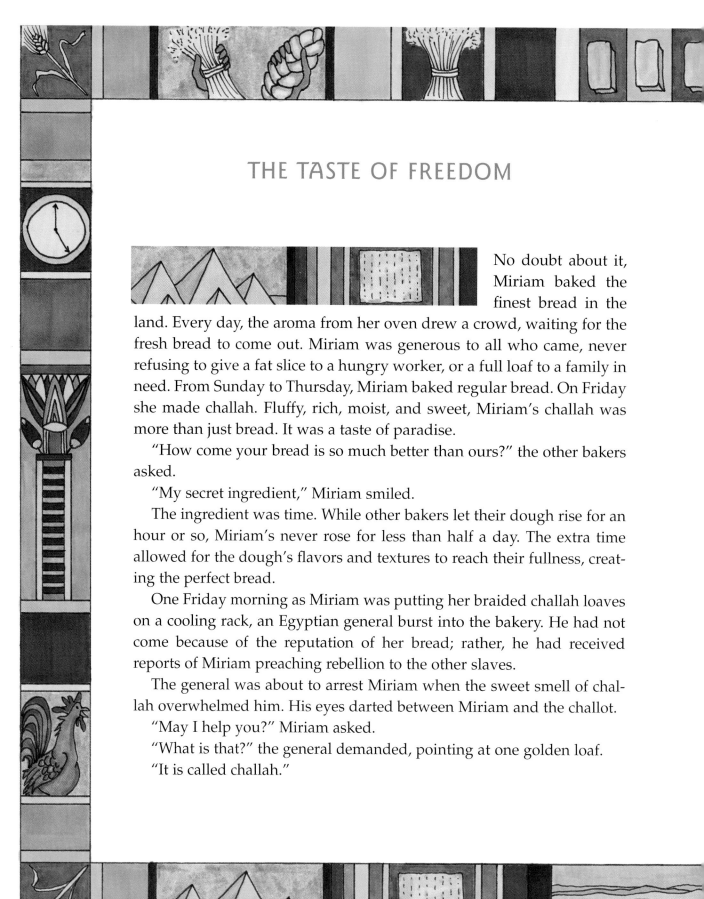

No doubt about it, Miriam baked the finest bread in the land. Every day, the aroma from her oven drew a crowd, waiting for the fresh bread to come out. Miriam was generous to all who came, never refusing to give a fat slice to a hungry worker, or a full loaf to a family in need. From Sunday to Thursday, Miriam baked regular bread. On Friday she made challah. Fluffy, rich, moist, and sweet, Miriam's challah was more than just bread. It was a taste of paradise.

"How come your bread is so much better than ours?" the other bakers asked.

"My secret ingredient," Miriam smiled.

The ingredient was time. While other bakers let their dough rise for an hour or so, Miriam's never rose for less than half a day. The extra time allowed for the dough's flavors and textures to reach their fullness, creating the perfect bread.

One Friday morning as Miriam was putting her braided challah loaves on a cooling rack, an Egyptian general burst into the bakery. He had not come because of the reputation of her bread; rather, he had received reports of Miriam preaching rebellion to the other slaves.

The general was about to arrest Miriam when the sweet smell of challah overwhelmed him. His eyes darted between Miriam and the challot.

"May I help you?" Miriam asked.

"What is that?" the general demanded, pointing at one golden loaf.

"It is called challah."

Miriam cut a piece for the general. He put the bread in his mouth and promptly forgot the reason he had come. He looked at her and announced, "Every Friday you will have fifty loaves of this challah delivered to Pharaoh."

The general turned and left.

"Fifty loaves?" Miriam moaned. "Where will I find the time?"

But an Israelite slave could not disobey an Egyptian order, so Miriam rolled up her sleeves. Early Friday morning before her rooster sang, Miriam was kneading dough. As the sun set on the day, Miriam finished loading the loaves into a wagon.

"My beautiful challot have become the bread of slavery," Miriam groaned as she watched two slaves wheel the wagon toward Pharaoh's palace.

Several months later, Miriam's younger brother, Moses, returned from exile to prophesy God's words of freedom to the Hebrew slaves.

"*Adonai*, the God of the Hebrews, will rescue you from Egypt," Moses preached. Miriam listened and shook her head.

Afterward, Moses asked, "Why did you shake your head? Do you prefer slavery over freedom?"

"No, brother," she answered. "It's just that I don't believe deliverance will come from God alone. We must help in the fight for our freedom."

"Have you no faith? Is not *Adonai* the God who created the heavens and earth? Does *Adonai* need our help? Is there anything under the sun in which *Adonai* needs the help of man?"

As it happened, Miriam was holding a bundle of wheat in one hand and a loaf of bread in the other.

"Tell me, brother, does this work of *Adonai*'s," she shook the wheat, "need the help of *woman* to create this?" She held up the bread.

Moses bowed before his sister.

"It is a great lesson you have taught, my sister. Clearly we are partners with God in our struggle. God has provided us the hope of becoming a free people and the strength to break the bonds of slavery. It is up to us to transform the hope and strength into freedom."

Moses, Miriam, and their brother Aaron worked hard to lead the Hebrews to freedom. With God's help, they succeeded. Pharaoh finally agreed to let the Hebrews go. Moses, however, was afraid that the fickle Pharaoh would change his mind, so the moment Pharaoh gave his consent to Moses, Moses commanded the Hebrews to pack their belongings and leave immediately.

When word came to go, Miriam and the bakers had just finished kneading the dough for the next day's bread. Though the dough had not yet risen, Miriam knew that they would need to eat as they escaped into the desert. There was no choice but to bake the unleavened dough. The other bakers followed her lead.

The bread that came out of the ovens was flat and crunchy, not fluffy and soft. Miriam called it "matzah."

As the Hebrews hiked through the desert, they ate the matzah. Even though it had not risen, something about the matzah made it the best bread they had ever tasted.

The Hebrew bakers gathered around Miriam.

"How can it be that this unleavened matzah tastes better than even your finest challah?"

Miriam smiled. "What you taste is the secret ingredient that none of our other loaves ever possessed: freedom."

And every year since then, when Jews celebrate their deliverance from Egypt at Passover, they bake a special bread of remembrance: matzah, the bread of freedom.

WHEAT

Wheat is appropriately called "the staff of life." It is the world's most important food crop, being the main staple of more than two billion people. From breakfast cereal, to sandwich bread, to pasta, to pie crust, wheat-based foods are common to people throughout much of the world.

Wheat is also a major source of animal feed. In addition, the stem of wheat, straw, has multiple uses. It is used for animal bedding and fuel, and when mixed with mud, it makes a material strong enough with which to build a house.

The history of wheat is the history of civilization. Native to the Middle East, wheat was perhaps the first plant ever cultivated, dating back twelve thousand years. People discovered that by growing wheat, they no longer needed to migrate to follow their food supplies. Instead, they could remain in one place and farm. When farmers found they could grow more wheat than they could eat, the surplus food freed some people to develop nonfarming skills, thereby laying the foundation for civilization.

Today, bread and salt are traditional Jewish gifts given when people move into a new home. The bread is given so that they will never know want, the salt so that their lives will be flavorful.

Two thousand years ago Rabbi Elazar ben Azariah summed up the relationship between humans and wheat when he said, "If there is no flour, there is no Torah; if there is no Torah, there is no flour" (*Pirkei Avot* 3:17). In other words, our spiritual and physical well-being are wedded together. We need both to be fully human.

On Friday nights, many Jews place two challah loaves on their Shabbat tables. The second loaf signifies the extra portion of manna God sent to the Israelites on Shabbat (Exodus 16:29). In the spirit of the second loaf, two stories about wheat are included in this book.

World's Best Challah (No Kidding)

Makes one loaf.

1 package yeast	¼ c. sugar
1 c. warm water	½ c. canola oil
1 Tbsp. honey	1 beaten egg
2 tsp. salt	3½ c. flour

Dissolve yeast in water and honey. When foam appears on the water's surface add salt, sugar, oil, and egg. Add most of the flour and mix until smooth. Slowly add the rest of the flour. Turn out onto a lightly floured board and knead until smooth, adding additional flour as needed until dough no longer sticks to fingers. Place in a bowl and cover with a clean, damp cloth. Let the dough rise in a warm place until it doubles in size (at least an hour). Punch it down and let it rise again another hour or more. (If you don't have the time for the second rising, it will still be good.) After punching it down a second time, cut into 3 equal sections and roll into snakes. Braid the snakes and bake at 350° for 35–50 minutes until golden brown.

Olive

THE CRYING TREE

There was a debate in the ancient Land of Israel as to which plant was the most honored. Some claimed it had to be either Barley or Wheat. After all, it was from these two grains that bread, the staff of life, was made. Others disagreed and said that the most honored plant must be one of those that produced the delicious fruit the land was famous for: Pomegranate, Fig, Grape, or Date. After days of debate, an agreement was reached—the most honored plant in Israel was Olive, a tree that made only a bitter fruit.

Upon hearing the decision, the six other sacred species protested. Date said to Olive, "No way can you be more honored than I. I'm five times taller than you." Olive looked up at Date and replied, "Did your height help Dove find a sign of life after the Flood waters receded?"

Wheat puffed out its grain and declared, "The bread placed before the ark in the Holy Temple is made from my flour." Olive quickly deflated Wheat with the words, "And by whose light did you find your way to the ark? It was oil made from me that kept the *Ner Tamid*, the Eternal Light, lit."

Grape attacked Olive. "I don't know why you think you are so honored. I'm every bit as honored as you. Kings use my wine to bless the Sabbath." Without a moment's hesitation Olive retorted, "And how was David made king? How was Solomon made king? They were anointed with *my* oil. And I'll tell you one more thing. All of Israel is waiting for the

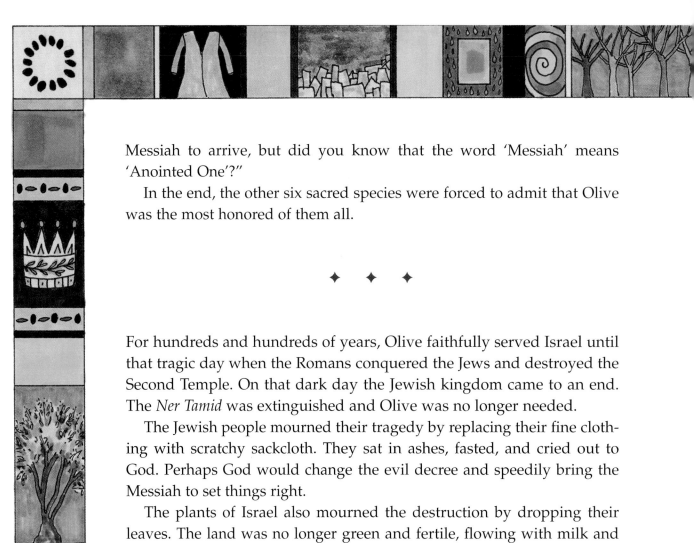

Messiah to arrive, but did you know that the word 'Messiah' means 'Anointed One'?"

In the end, the other six sacred species were forced to admit that Olive was the most honored of them all.

◆   ◆   ◆

For hundreds and hundreds of years, Olive faithfully served Israel until that tragic day when the Romans conquered the Jews and destroyed the Second Temple. On that dark day the Jewish kingdom came to an end. The *Ner Tamid* was extinguished and Olive was no longer needed.

The Jewish people mourned their tragedy by replacing their fine clothing with scratchy sackcloth. They sat in ashes, fasted, and cried out to God. Perhaps God would change the evil decree and speedily bring the Messiah to set things right.

The plants of Israel also mourned the destruction by dropping their leaves. The land was no longer green and fertile, flowing with milk and honey. It was brown and lifeless. In all the Land of Israel there was only one tree whose leaves remained on its branches: Olive.

Word quickly spread that proud Olive was too vain, too uncaring to mourn the disaster that had befallen the Jewish nation.

Olive said, "It is not so that I do not mourn. Who but God can look inside and measure a being's suffering?"

The plants were unmoved. "All of Israel sits in sackcloth and ashes. We have all shed our leaves, while you stand tall and proud, as if nothing happened, as if the Temple still stood, as if our kings still reigned."

Olive replied, "Some mourn on the outside and it is easy to see their tears. Others cry inside. Look closely and you can see that my tears are shed from within.

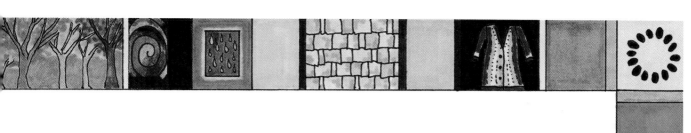

"Yes, my leaves and my fruit remain. They remain for one purpose. They remain in the hope that the Messiah will come speedily in our day. When the Messiah comes, my oil will be ready to anoint him or her. Perhaps the Messiah will desire a garland of leaves to signal to the world that peace has arrived."

The plants had to agree that Olive spoke truth.

Eventually, the leaves returned to the plants of Israel. The only tree still shedding tears for the destruction that took place two thousand years ago is Olive.

To this day, olive trees do not hold themselves tall and proud. As they age, their tears hollow out their insides, making them gnarled and bent over.

Thus they will remain until the Messiah arrives and Olive will once again be called upon to serve Israel.

THE OLIVE

Olives are some of the world's longest living trees. Since they can attain an age of two thousand years, it is possible that some trees in Israel witnessed the Roman conquest in 70 c.e. While the olive does not grow higher than twenty-five feet, an older tree can have a circumference of twenty feet. Four adults holding hands would barely reach around the trunk of a thousand-year-old olive tree.

While olives are a delicacy treasured throughout the world, ripe olives cannot be eaten directly off the tree. They must be treated to rid the fruit of their bitterness. The majority of olives are grown for their oil. Olive oil is reputed to be one of the finest and healthiest plant-based oils. It is little wonder that olive oil was used throughout the biblical era to anoint kings (I Samuel 16:13) and priests (Exodus 28–29), as well as to light the *Ner Tamid* in the Temple (Exodus 27:20). The miracle of Chanukah (B. Talmud *Shabbat* 21b) occurred when one cruse of olive oil, a single day's supply, kept the menorah lit for eight days during the Temple rededication ceremony following Judah Maccabee's victory over the Greco-Syrians.

The production of olive oil is a process that has not dramatically changed since the days of Jewish kings and priests. Olives are gathered and set in the sun for eight to ten days. This allows most of the water in the olives to evaporate. The olives are then crushed between heavy stone mills to release the oil that is contained in both the flesh and the seed. The mixture is placed in an olive press where a powerful screw presses out the oil. Gentle pressure is applied at first to yield the best oil, called "virgin." Then the mixture is pressed harder, yielding a lower quality oil. A final pressing creates "olive residue," which is used in the making of soaps, cosmetics, and medicines.

The hard olive wood is used by craftspeople in Israel to make a number of religious ritual items such as candlesticks, *etrog* holders, and *Havdalah* spice boxes.

The olive tree is important not only for the products that come from it, but also for its symbolic value. From the time the dove brought Noah leaves from an olive tree, the olive branch has been a symbol of peace. In fact, to demonstrate its role as world peacekeeper, the United Nations chose as its flag a map of the world surrounded by two olive branches. Truly, the olive is a much honored tree.

Curing Olives

Curing olives is easy, fun, and delicious. First, find an olive tree with black olives on it. Olives usually ripen between November and March. Use unbruised olives. (It is best to pick olives from the trees, rather than using those that have fallen to the ground.) To leach out the bitterness, prick each olive with a knife and place the olives in a brine solution (¼ c. of pickling salt to 1 qt. of water). Be sure that all the olives are covered by the brine. Change the solution once a week. The olives should be ready to eat in five to seven weeks.

Pistachio Stuffed Olives

Buy the largest, fresh, pitted black olives you can find. Do not use canned. Stuff each olive with a shelled pistachio nut. The stuffed olives can be stored in the refrigerator for up to five days in a sealed container.

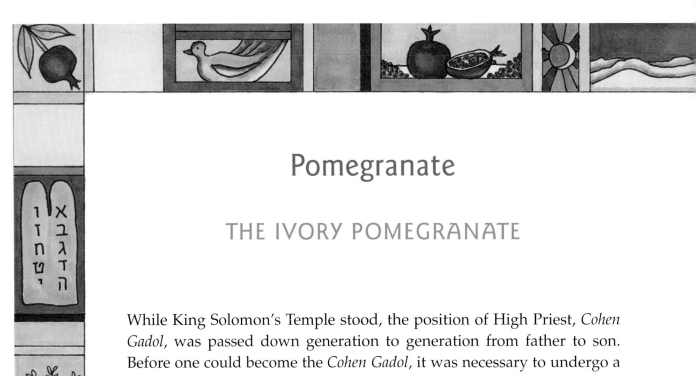

Pomegranate

THE IVORY POMEGRANATE

While King Solomon's Temple stood, the position of High Priest, *Cohen Gadol*, was passed down generation to generation from father to son. Before one could become the *Cohen Gadol*, it was necessary to undergo a long and rigorous priestly training.

It was time for Eliahu to begin his training. Eliahu was an inquisitive boy. Never satisfied with what he was taught, Eliahu needed to discover truth for himself.

For example, when Eliahu was taught that birds fly south for the winter in order to stay warm, he caught a bird at the start of the winter migration. Each day as the air grew colder, he watched the bird. The morning he saw the bird shivering, Eliahu gave it an extra portion of seed, then opened the cage and watched the bird fly south, satisfied that he had discovered truth for himself.

On the first day of his priestly studies, Eliahu said, "Father, you have taught me much about God, but I have found no evidence that proves God's existence. I cannot train to be *Cohen Gadol* until I have discovered for myself that there is a God."

"Son, you have an unquenchable thirst for truth," his father said. "If you observe closely, you will find many proofs of God's existence woven into the glorious fabric of Creation."

"Where?" asked Eliahu.

His father's eyes swept across the room and fell upon a bowl of pome-

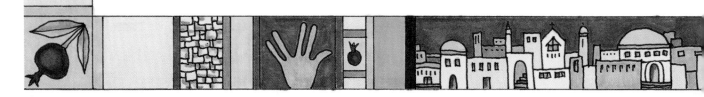

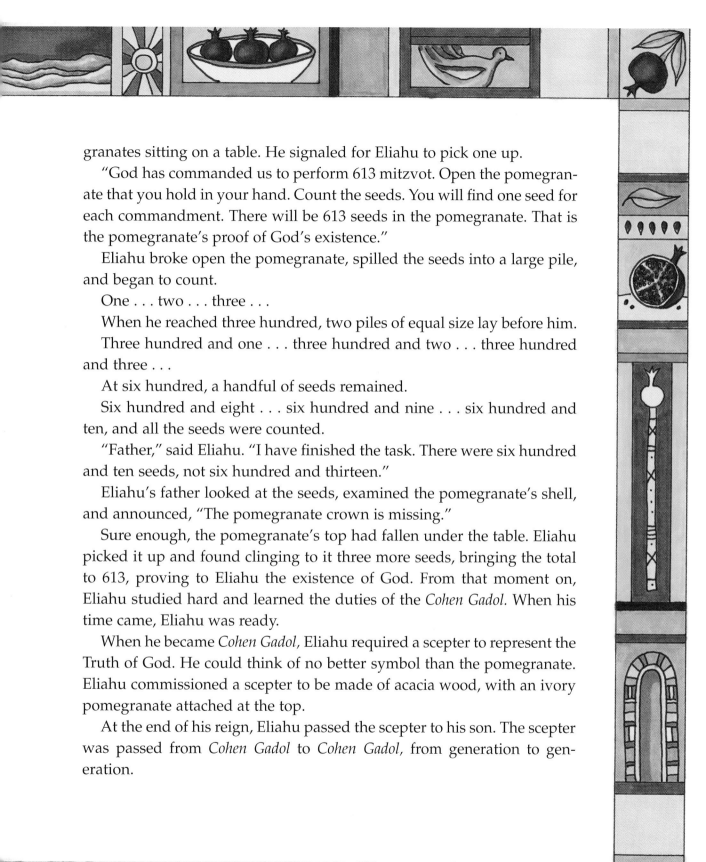

granates sitting on a table. He signaled for Eliahu to pick one up.

"God has commanded us to perform 613 mitzvot. Open the pomegranate that you hold in your hand. Count the seeds. You will find one seed for each commandment. There will be 613 seeds in the pomegranate. That is the pomegranate's proof of God's existence."

Eliahu broke open the pomegranate, spilled the seeds into a large pile, and began to count.

One . . . two . . . three . . .

When he reached three hundred, two piles of equal size lay before him.

Three hundred and one . . . three hundred and two . . . three hundred and three . . .

At six hundred, a handful of seeds remained.

Six hundred and eight . . . six hundred and nine . . . six hundred and ten, and all the seeds were counted.

"Father," said Eliahu. "I have finished the task. There were six hundred and ten seeds, not six hundred and thirteen."

Eliahu's father looked at the seeds, examined the pomegranate's shell, and announced, "The pomegranate crown is missing."

Sure enough, the pomegranate's top had fallen under the table. Eliahu picked it up and found clinging to it three more seeds, bringing the total to 613, proving to Eliahu the existence of God. From that moment on, Eliahu studied hard and learned the duties of the *Cohen Gadol.* When his time came, Eliahu was ready.

When he became *Cohen Gadol,* Eliahu required a scepter to represent the Truth of God. He could think of no better symbol than the pomegranate. Eliahu commissioned a scepter to be made of acacia wood, with an ivory pomegranate attached at the top.

At the end of his reign, Eliahu passed the scepter to his son. The scepter was passed from *Cohen Gadol* to *Cohen Gadol,* from generation to generation.

✦ ✦ ✦

Two hundred and fifty years after Eliahu's death, the Babylonians conquered the Land of Israel and attacked Jerusalem. Their soldiers broke into the sacred Temple grounds and slaughtered priests as they raced toward their goal, the Temple's most sacred spot, the Holiest of Holies, the chamber where the tablets of the Ten Commandments were kept.

At the entrance of the chamber stood Seraiah, the *Cohen Gadol*. Seraiah cried to the attackers, "By the Truth of God, do not touch this sacred chamber."

Seraiah held the scepter between himself and his attackers. With one sword swipe, the ivory pomegranate was severed from the staff.

Seraiah spoke again, "You can kill me and destroy the Temple, but you will never destroy the Truth of God. In the end, the Babylonians will disappear and the Jews will triumph."

The Babylonians laughed and a soldier ran a spear through Seraiah.

Two thousand five hundred years later, Seraiah's prophesy has come to pass. The Babylonians have disappeared, and the Jews have returned to the Land of Israel to rebuild their nation. In the 1970's an ancient ivory pomegranate mysteriously appeared in a Jerusalem antique shop. Engraved on the small pomegranate were the words, "Sacred to the priests in the House of God." Archaeologists determined that the pomegranate came from King Solomon's Temple. Whether or not it once was part of the *Cohen Gadol*'s scepter is unknown, yet this ivory pomegranate is the only surviving relic from Solomon's Temple ever found. It can be seen on display at the Israel Museum in Jerusalem.

THE POMEGRANATE

 With its spindly branches the pomegranate resembles not so much a tree as a large bush. Yet the ten-to twenty-five-foot tree is hardy and can live for up to two hundred years. Originally from the semi-arid region of Persia, the pomegranate requires little water to grow.

The pomegranate's red fruit is topped by what looks like a crown. Perhaps royal crowns of antiquity were influenced by this beautiful fruit. Inside the pomegranate are hundreds of red edible seeds. While not every pomegranate contains 613 seeds, the average ranges between five and eight hundred.

The fruit ripens in late summer. If left on the trees, the fruit will crack, exposing the seeds hidden inside. The seeds are dispersed when birds eat them, digesting the sweet and nutritious covering while passing the seeds through their digestive tracts.

If pomegranates are picked before they crack, they can be kept for many months. In fact, the fruit improves with age. In ancient times, desert caravans would carry pomegranates for their thirst-quenching juice.

Pomegranates are mentioned in the Torah as one of the fruits brought back by the spies as proof of the land's fertility (Numbers 13:23). Pomegranate designs were sewn on the hem of Aaron's priestly robe (Exodus 28:34). In Solomon's Temple, the tops of the pillars were carved with pomegranate images (I Kings 7:18).

Jewish tradition compares a good pupil to a pomegranate (B. Talmud *Chagigah* 15b). The delicious seeds of the pomegranate are embedded in an inedible rind. In the same manner, a good student is able to glean the important gems in his or her studies and discard that which is unimportant.

The pomegranate is also found in ancient Greek culture. It was known as a fertility fruit. Some scholars believe that it was the fruit Paris gave to Aphrodite, thereby launching the Trojan War.

In addition to its edible seeds, the pomegranate has other uses. The rind can be made into a dark brown dye. The pomegranate can be cut in half and juiced with a citrus juicer. Grenadine, a popular mixing drink, is made from pomegranate juice.

Festive Fall Salad with Pomegranate Seeds

⅓ pound arugula
1 small head of red leaf or other
    lettuce
½ c. pomegranate seeds
½ c. walnut pieces, toasted

1 avocado, diced
½ c. feta cheese, crumbled
2 or 3 cooked beets, diced and
    chilled

Pomegranate Citrus Vinaigrette

Note: Recipe makes enough vinaigrette for about 2–3 salads.

½ c. oil (olive or canola)
2 cloves of garlic, pressed or finely
    diced
1 shallot, finely diced
Juice of 1 orange or ¼ c. orange
    juice
1 Tbsp. lemon juice

¼ c. rice wine vinegar
1 Tbsp. basalmic vinegar
2 Tbsp. pomegranate juice or syrup
1 tsp. salt
¼ tsp. pepper
1 tsp. sugar (optional)

Tear the lettuce and arugula and place in a large bowl. Add beets and all remaining ingredients. Immediately before serving, add the vinaigrette and toss.

Barley

BARLEY BROTHERS

 Once upon a time, a man owned a large field. Before he died he built a stone wall through the middle, to divide the land equally between his two sons. One son was married and supported a family of eight children. The other was single and lived by himself.

It was the end of the barley harvest. The brothers had helped each other cut and stack the barley against the stone wall. One brother's barley lay on his side of the wall. The second brother's barley lay on the other side.

That night the married brother stayed up late.

"My poor brother," he said to himself. "When I am old and no longer able to farm, my children will care for me and my wife. Yet my brother is all alone. Who will take care of him when he no longer has the strength to farm?"

The brother thought awhile longer and decided upon a plan.

"This year God has blessed me with a bountiful crop. My family will not be able to eat it all. I will take some of my barley and put it on my brother's side of the fence. That way he will have more barley to sell."

The brother went to his barley stack. He took a few bushels of barley and dumped them over the side of the wall onto his brother's barley. He then went home, anticipating the look of surprise on his brother's face when he discovered the extra barley.

That same night, the single brother could not sleep.

"I am worried about my brother," he said to himself. "Here I am with

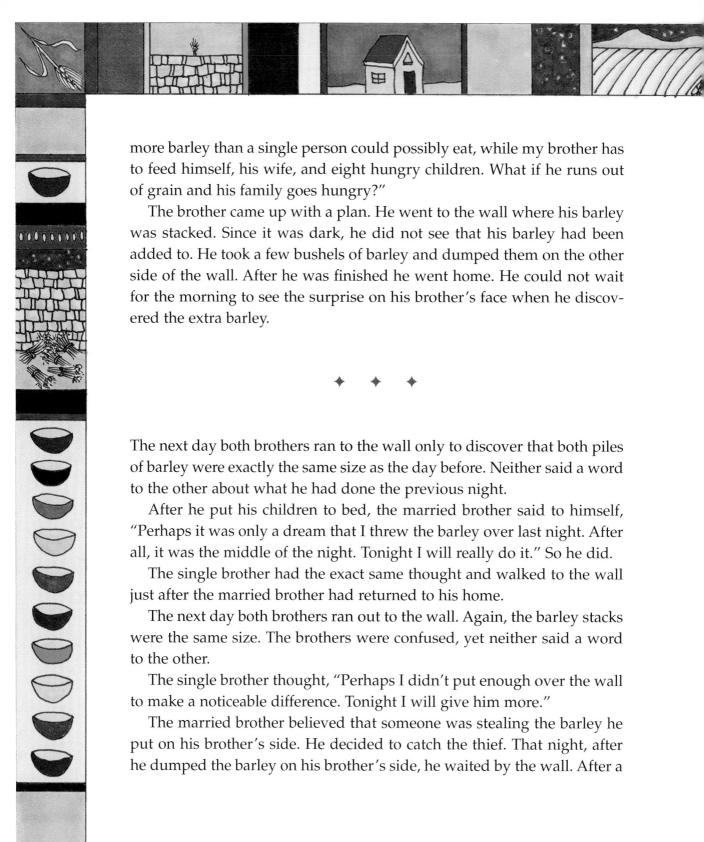

more barley than a single person could possibly eat, while my brother has to feed himself, his wife, and eight hungry children. What if he runs out of grain and his family goes hungry?"

The brother came up with a plan. He went to the wall where his barley was stacked. Since it was dark, he did not see that his barley had been added to. He took a few bushels of barley and dumped them on the other side of the wall. After he was finished he went home. He could not wait for the morning to see the surprise on his brother's face when he discovered the extra barley.

◆　◆　◆

The next day both brothers ran to the wall only to discover that both piles of barley were exactly the same size as the day before. Neither said a word to the other about what he had done the previous night.

After he put his children to bed, the married brother said to himself, "Perhaps it was only a dream that I threw the barley over last night. After all, it was the middle of the night. Tonight I will really do it." So he did.

The single brother had the exact same thought and walked to the wall just after the married brother had returned to his home.

The next day both brothers ran out to the wall. Again, the barley stacks were the same size. The brothers were confused, yet neither said a word to the other.

The single brother thought, "Perhaps I didn't put enough over the wall to make a noticeable difference. Tonight I will give him more."

The married brother believed that someone was stealing the barley he put on his brother's side. He decided to catch the thief. That night, after he dumped the barley on his brother's side, he waited by the wall. After a couple of minutes he heard footsteps. He saw a sheaf of barley being raised above the wall. At that moment, he sprang over the wall and tackled the thief.

When he lifted the thief to his feet, he saw his brother. Instantly, both men realized what had happened. They hugged each other, and the next morning they tore down the wall that divided the field.

God, who had been watching these events, decreed, "I have searched the world for a place of true brotherly love, a place to put my precious Temple. My search is over. The Temple will be built here."

And so it was that years later, King Solomon built the Holy Temple on this field of barley.

BARLEY

Sometime between 9000 and 5000 B.C.E., barley became one of the first crops cultivated by humans. Barley was the main staple food in the ancient Middle East. While the quality of bread made from barley is lower than that of wheat, it was more widely grown because it can grow in poorer soils. In fact, only kings, priests, and the wealthy ate wheat bread on a daily basis.

Today barley accounts for 10 percent of all grain produced in the world. (This compares to wheat, which accounts for 25 percent.) Barley has two main uses. About one-half of the annual barley harvest is used for animal feed. The remaining half is sprouted and dried to produce malt. Malt is the primary ingredient in beer and whiskey production.

Barley ripens before wheat. The spring holiday Passover coincides with the beginning of the barley harvest. The two harvests are connected to each other through the counting of the *Omer* (barley sheaves). The counting takes forty-nine days. When the counting is finished, the barley harvest ends and the wheat harvest begins. The holiday of Shavuot celebrates this day (Leviticus 23:5–21). The Book of Ruth, whose story takes place during the barley harvest, is the biblical book read at Shavuot.

Barley plays a significant role in the biblical story of Gideon. The story explains how the nomadic Midianites stole the Israelites' crops year after year. God chose Gideon to lead a rebellion against the oppressive Midianites. God wanted it to be known throughout the land that the Israelite victory would be due to God's power and not to the power of the Israelites. Therefore, God allowed Gideon only three hundred soldiers to fight the tens of thousands of Midianites. Sensing Gideon's fear, God sent him to overhear a conversation between two Midianite guards. One guard related a dream about a loaf of barley bread whirling through the Midianite camp, overturning a tent. The second guard interpreted the dream to mean that the agriculturally based Israelites (the barley bread) were going to overthrow the nomadic Midianites (the tent). Indeed, that was exactly what later happened (Judges 7:13).

Mushroom Barley Soup

3 Tbsp. oil

2 onions, diced

4 stalks celery, sliced

1½ pounds crimini or white mushrooms, diced

4–5 carrots, sliced

3 cloves garlic, pressed or finely chopped

1 tsp. ground cumin

1½ tsp. sea salt, plus more to taste

ground pepper to taste

15 c. water or stock (if using water, add approximately 4 cubes of bouillon)

1½ c. barley

In a large soup pot, heat oil. Sauté the onions and celery for 5 minutes. Add the mushrooms, carrots, garlic, cumin, salt, and pepper. Sauté on medium heat for 5 minutes or until the mushrooms release their water. Make sure that the temperature is not so high that the liquid cooks away.

Add the stock and bring to a low boil. Add the barley and simmer 45 minutes or until the barley is plump and soft.

Before serving, taste the soup and add more bouillon, salt, or pepper if needed.

Grape

KIDDUSH

A story is told of the first Friday afternoon. After working nonstop for six days, God had completed the heavens and earth. Now it was time to relax. God instructed Adam and Eve to prepare a ceremony to begin Shabbat, the day of rest.

"Nothing too fancy," said God.

So the first couple decided on three items for the ceremony: Candle, Challah, and Wine.

"Light, food, and drink," said Adam. "I think we picked well. We can bless each item and then Shabbat will begin."

"Agreed," said Eve. "But Shabbat itself needs to be blessed. To which of the three should the honor be given?"

"With me!" Candle, Challah, and Wine shouted in unison. A noisy ruckus ensued, with each item boasting of its particular attributes.

Eve held up her hand. "One at a time, please."

"Certainly," said Candle, stretching itself to its full height. "It is perfectly clear why *I* should be chosen to bless the sacred Shabbat. Was not light God's first act of Creation?"

Candle looked to see if the other items were paying attention.

"Shabbat begins when I'm lit. Clearly, I'm the most important. Therefore, logically, the Shabbat blessing must be made through me.

"And I have even more to say about me," Candle continued,"My fire provides the warmth and energy needed for safety, comfort, and last but certainly not least, cooking."

Candle stuck its wick straight up into the air and was done.

"Pshaw!" snickered Challah, weaving its way in front of the candle. "Who easily loses control and obliterates everything in its path? That's right, Candle, I'm talking to you. Go ahead and glare, but you know it's the truth."

Presenting a fat raisin to Adam, Challah gracefully bowed and said, "It is I, your most humble servant Challah, whom Shabbat should be blessed through. Am I not the staff of life? Without food, not a single living creature could exist. After all, everyone from the lowly gnat to the exalted human must eat.

"Yet, there is more," Challah continued. "In the future when the Children of Israel wander through the desert, God will teach them of Shabbat's bounty through the double portion of the bread-like manna."

"Hah!" Candle sparked. "In the future, you will be used as a weapon against the poor. The rich will become greedy and smug, and forget their responsibilities toward Creation and its creatures."

"Quiet, you stuck-up pile of paraffin!"

"Yeast breath!"

Candle and Challah were ready to fight.

Eve stepped between them and said, "Please, let's hear from Wine."

Wine slowly swished to the front and spoke with a slightly bent neck. "I am of little weight when compared to Candle's creative light or to the sustenance provided by Challah. I am not needed for survival. My only qualities are that I bring joy and relaxation."

Candle snorted, "When one drinks too much of you, it won't be joy and relaxation, but sickness that you'll bring."

"And danger," added Challah.

"That is true," Wine admitted.

The three became quiet.

Eve spoke first. "I agree with Candle. The blessing should be made over Candle."

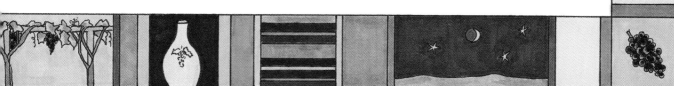

"I agree with Challah," Adam said. "The blessing should be made over Challah, especially Challah with raisins."

The humans argued back and forth, but could come to no agreement. They asked God to cast the deciding vote.

God said, "It is a difficult decision. Therefore, I think it best to ask what is the essence of the Shabbat that is to be blessed."

Eve said, "The essence of Shabbat is the joy in appreciating the beautiful Creation You have given us."

"Don't forget relaxation," said Adam. "After a hard workweek, we're going to need some rest."

God nodded, "I agree. Joy and relaxation are the essence of Shabbat."

"Candle doesn't provide either," said Adam.

"Neither does Challah," added Eve.

Everyone, including Challah and Candle, turned to Wine and understood God's wisdom. And so it came to pass that Adam and Eve sanctified the first Shabbat through Wine. And it has been that way ever since.

THE GRAPE

The grapevine is one of the fastest growing plants in the world. It can produce up to thirty feet of new growth in a single summer. Because it is a vine, the grape cannot support itself upright. To obtain the sunlight it needs, the grapevine uses other plants or artificial supports to climb.

A well-known biblical story about grapes involves the spies that Moses sent to the land of Canaan (Numbers 13:23). To demonstrate the fertility of the land, the spies brought back a single grape cluster so large that it needed to be carried by two men. This image is now the official symbol of Israel's Office of Tourism.

There are more than five thousand varieties of grapes. The vast majority of cultivated grapes are grown to make wine. The production of wine may have been the first or at least one of the earliest businesses in the world. Archaeologists have found evidence of a wine industry from as early as 3000 B.C.E.

Making wine is easy—stomp the grapes to break the fruit, add yeast to turn the sugars into alcohol, press the mixture to obtain the fermented juice, and bottle it. Learning to make *good* wine, however, is a difficult art to master.

The most important factor in wine production is the quality of the grape. To best control quality, farmers never raise grapevines from seed. Rather, canes, small cuttings taken from a high quality vine, are used to grow new grapevines. Many current varieties come from canes whose original vines were grown three hundred to thirteen hundred years ago!

The grape leaf can be used as an edible wrapper to make *dolmas,* called *alei-gefen* in Hebrew, a delicious Middle Eastern dish. In addition, the flexible canes can be woven into wreaths and baskets.

Wine was such an important part of Greek and Roman life that Greeks and Romans each had their own wine god, Dionysus and Bacchus. Rather than drinking wine undiluted (as is the case today), in ancient times wine was usually diluted with water. Spice, herb, or flower flavorings were added as preservatives and for medicinal purposes.

Judaism holds ambivalent views regarding wine. On one hand, Judaism recognizes that wine, in moderation, induces appetite, sustains, and makes glad (B. Talmud *B'rachot* 35b). Besides its use in Shabbat and other festivals, wine is an essential part of many Jewish rituals. An eight-day-old boy is given wine during his *b'rit milah.* A traditional gift to the *b'nai mitzvah* boy or girl is a *Kiddush* cup. The bride and groom share two glasses of wine as part of the wedding ceremony.

On the other hand, Judaism recognizes the problems caused by too much wine. One midrash explains, "As wine enters a man's body, it grows lax and his mind is confused. Once wine enters, reason leaves" (Numbers Rabbah 10:8). The Torah illustrates this point at the ending of the Noah story (Genesis 9:20–27). Following the Flood, Noah plants a vineyard, makes wine, and becomes drunk. While drunk, his son Ham does something evil to Noah. Noah curses him and his children. So the reborn world cleansed of sin by the Flood is quickly off to a bad beginning because of wine.

Unlike some other cultures and religions, Judaism does not use wine as a path to God. The first priests, Aaron and his sons, were warned never to enter God's sanctuary in a drunken state (Leviticus 10:8–9). Additionally, in ancient Israel the Nazirite spiritual seekers were not only forbidden wine, but also grapes (Numbers 6:4)! However, during Purim there is a custom where one is allowed to become so drunk that it is impossible to tell the difference between the evil Haman and the blessed Mordechai.

In the end, responsible wine drinking does have its place in the Jewish tradition as it brings joy and relaxation, feelings we need to have more of, especially on Shabbat.

Dolmas

30–40 grape leaves (large ones with fine veins)
juice of 1 lemon
1 c. water
3 Tbsp. olive oil
1 Tbsp. sugar
1 Tbsp. salt

Filling

3 Tbsp. olive oil
1 large onion, chopped
1 c. rice, washed
¼ c. pine nuts

1 Tbsp. salt
1 Tbsp. sugar
¼ c. currants
1 c. boiling water
½ bunch dill, mint, and parsley

For the filling, heat oil in a saucepan and cook onion until golden. Add washed, uncooked rice and pine nuts. Stir over medium heat for 30 minutes or until rice becomes golden in color. Add salt, sugar, currants. Add 1 c. boiling water, cover, and cook for 15 minutes on very low heat. Add dill, mint, and parsley.

   Remove stems from leaves and boil grape leaves for 5 minutes in 2 qts. water and lemon juice. Place 1 Tbsp. of filling in leaf, fold over sides, and roll toward tip of leaf. Place dolmas in casserole dish. Pour water, oil, sugar, and salt into the dish and cook at 325° for 30 minutes or until water is absorbed.

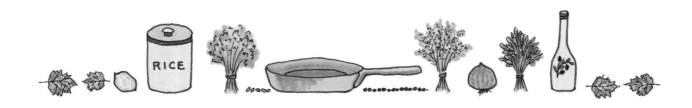

SOURCES

"The Teaching Date" is based on a folk custom that may have started in Tsfat's sixteenth-century kabbalistic community. Three-year-old males were given their first haircuts at a ceremony called an *upsherin*. The ceremony included giving the child sweets while introducing him to the study of Torah. Four hundred years later, many Jewish families have *upsherin* ceremonies to celebrate their child's third birthday and the beginning of Torah study. Leviticus Rabbah 7:3 explains why children should begin their Torah study with Leviticus.

"Not Yet" is loosely based on a story about the Messiah sitting among the lepers in Rome (B. Talmud *Sanhedrin* 98a). Rabbi Joshua greets the Messiah and asks, "When will you come?" The Messiah answers, "Today, if you will hear My voice." In both "Not Yet" and the original story, the Messiah/messianic age is here at hand, but is held up by imperfect human behavior. The comparison of a fig to the Torah can be found in the third section of the Tu BiSh'vat seder, originally developed by the Tsfat kabbalistic community.

There are many versions of "God Is Hungry." The original source may be Shivhai he-Ari (Tsfat, sixteenth-century), 24. The English language source is Bin Gorion I, 524–27.

"The Taste of Freedom" is not based on any source other than the supposition by some scholars that Miriam was more involved with the Exodus than the Bible relates.

"The Crying Tree" is an original story.

"The Ivory Pomegranate" is not based on any source other than the actual ivory pomegranate, which is on display at the Israel Museum.

"Barley Brothers" is one of the most beloved stories in the Jewish tradition. It can be found in Midrash Leviticus Rabbah 13 and *Mikveh Israel* (Israel Kosta, 1851), #89.

The inspiration for "Kiddush" came after a glass of Marr Vineyards Zinfandel, 1999.